I Can Read!™

BEGINNING
1
READING

Roary's Birthday Surprise

HarperCollins Children's Books

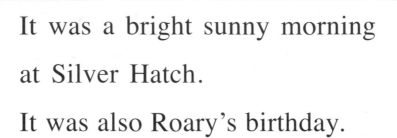

It was a bright sunny morning at Silver Hatch.

It was also Roary's birthday.

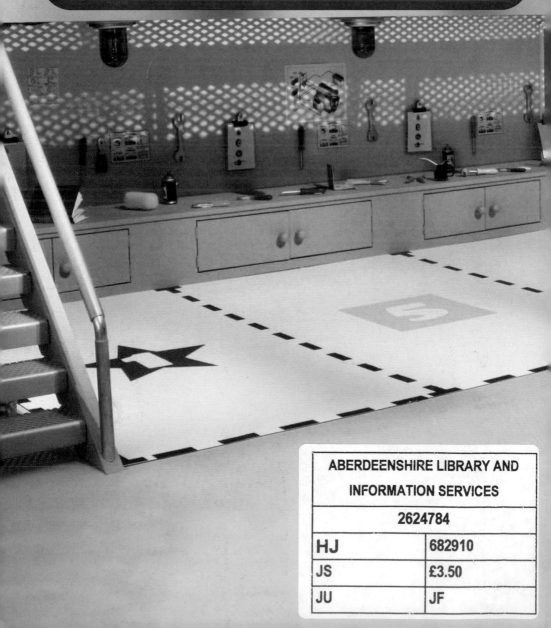

Dear Parent:
Your child's love of reading starts here!

Every child learns to read in a different way and at his or her own speed. Some go back and forth between reading levels and read favourite books again and again. Others read through each level in order. You can help your young reader improve and become more confident by encouraging his or her own interests and abilities. From books your child reads with you to the first books he or she reads alone, there are I Can Read Books for every stage of reading:

SHARED READING
Basic language, word repetition, and whimsical illustrations, ideal for sharing with your emergent reader

BEGINNING READING
Short sentences, familiar words, and simple concepts for children eager to read on their own

READING WITH HELP
Engaging stories, longer sentences, and language play for developing readers

READING ALONE
Complex plots, challenging vocabulary, and high-interest topics for the independent reader

ADVANCED READING
Short paragraphs, chapters, and exciting themes for the perfect bridge to chapter books

I Can Read Books have introduced children to the joy of reading since 1957. Featuring award-winning authors and illustrators and a fabulous cast of beloved characters, I Can Read Books set the standard for beginning readers.

A lifetime of discovery begins with the magical words **"I Can Read!"**

Roary's Birthday Surprise

First published in the UK by HarperCollins Children's Books in 2008
HarperCollins Children's Books is a division of HarperCollins Publishers Ltd.

1 3 5 7 9 10 8 6 4 2

ISBN-13: 978-0-00-727517-5
ISBN-10: 0-00-727517-X

© Chapman Entertainment Limited & David Jenkins 2008
www.roarytheracingcar.com

A CIP catalogue for this title is available from the British Library.

Printed and bound in China

Roary was very happy.

It was his first birthday
at Silver Hatch
and Roary could not wait
to see all of his friends.

"I'll go and see Big Chris first,"
Roary said.

"Morning, Roary," Big Chris said.

He was busy working on Maxi.

"How are you today?"

8

"I'm really happy!" Roary said.

"Why is that, son?"

asked Big Chris.

Roary could not believe it.

Big Chris had forgotten his birthday!

Next, Roary went to visit Cici.

She would not forget his birthday.

The little pink car
was doing her laps.

"Ello Roary," she said. "Racc me?"

"Oh yes!" Roary smiled.

The two little cars
sped around the track.
Roary tried his best
but Cici was just too fast!

"I thought you might let me win today," Roary said.

"Why?" Cici asked.

"Is today important?"

Not Cici as well!

Had everyone forgotten his birthday?

Roary drove away sadly.

"Maybe Flash has remembered

my birthday," he thought.

"Hey, Roary!" Flash was sitting

outside his burrow.

"Are you excited?" said Flash

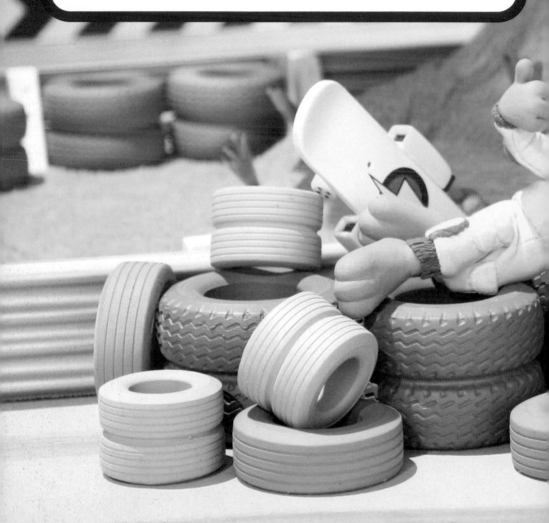

"I knew you wouldn't forget!"
Roary said. He was very happy.

"How could I forget the big race?"
Flash laughed.

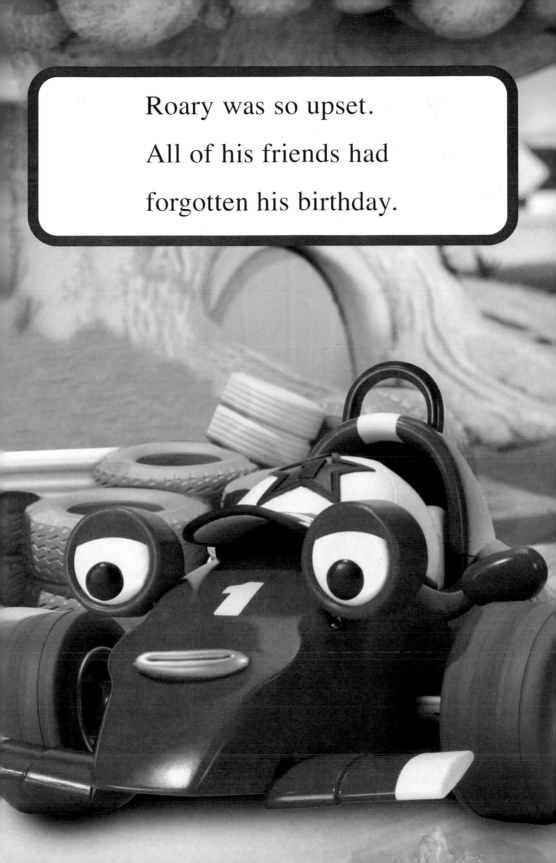

Roary was so upset.
All of his friends had
forgotten his birthday.

"Come on, Roary," Flash said.

"Let's go and see Big Chris.

You need new tyres."

Roary followed Flash

back to the garage.

Roary could not believe it.

All of his friends were there!

26

"Happy birthday, Roary!" everyone said.

27

Cici gave Roary a birthday hat.

"Blow out your candles and make a wish," Flash said.

"I wish to have all of my birthdays with my friends at Silver Hatch," Roary said.

31

Race to the finish line with these fun story and activity books.

Roary the Racing Car is out now on DVD!

Rev up R/C Roary to race to victory!

Start your engines with Talking Big Chris!

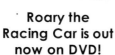

Go Roary, go-oooo!

Get rea to race

Light ' up Roa

Visit Roary at www.roarytheracingcar.com